FLIGHT

The strong and fearless rocker gorilla. Although he is really big and hairy, this gorilla is a gentle giant. You know Flight is ready for air time when you hear him grunt **"OOOHHHH, OOOHHHH, OOOHHHH!"**

Dazzle

The tough and brave bear who is a tomboy at heart. The boys can't keep up with Dazzle and good luck trying to slow her down! She has a big grin, and you will often hear her friendly growl, **"GRRRRR!"**

D1119534

MISCHIEF

The joker who is always up to something sneaky. He's a little short for a wolf, so be careful you don't confuse him with a fox. When Mischief is excited, you will hear him howl, **"aaaaWHOOOOO!"**

While Leap slept, Santa was busy delivering presents. He was almost done. X-ville was the only town left, but he struggled through the snow storm.

"Steady, Rudolph! Easy, Cupid! Relax, Vixen!" commanded Santa. "Oh no. I'm losing my grip. Oh dear. Oh dear. Oh reindeer!"

Meanwhile, the sounds of Christmas filled the air—

CRACKLING, CRINKLING, AND CRUNCHING.

It was the X-ville Christmas Eve Masher—the only monster truck show in the snow. The X-tails never missed it.

Launching off the high jump, Charm the Kangaroo sang out loud.
♪♪ "Tis the season to be jumping. Fa, la, la, la, la—la, la, la, la!" ♪♪

Crash the Hippo shouted his favorite song.
♪♪ "JINGLE BELLS, JINGLE BELLS, JINGLE ALL
THE WAY! OH WHAT FUN IT IS TO RIDE IN
A MONSTER TRUCK TODAY! HEY!" ♪♪

After lots of mashing, Mischief the Wolf PancakeD the last car. The monster truck show was over.

"Look," squealed Charm, "I won a present for the highest jump! I was told it's a magic present and I'm not to open it until Christmas morning. What could it be?"

"It's probably coal," grinned Mischief.

"If it's coal, then I've got your present by mistake," giggled Charm.

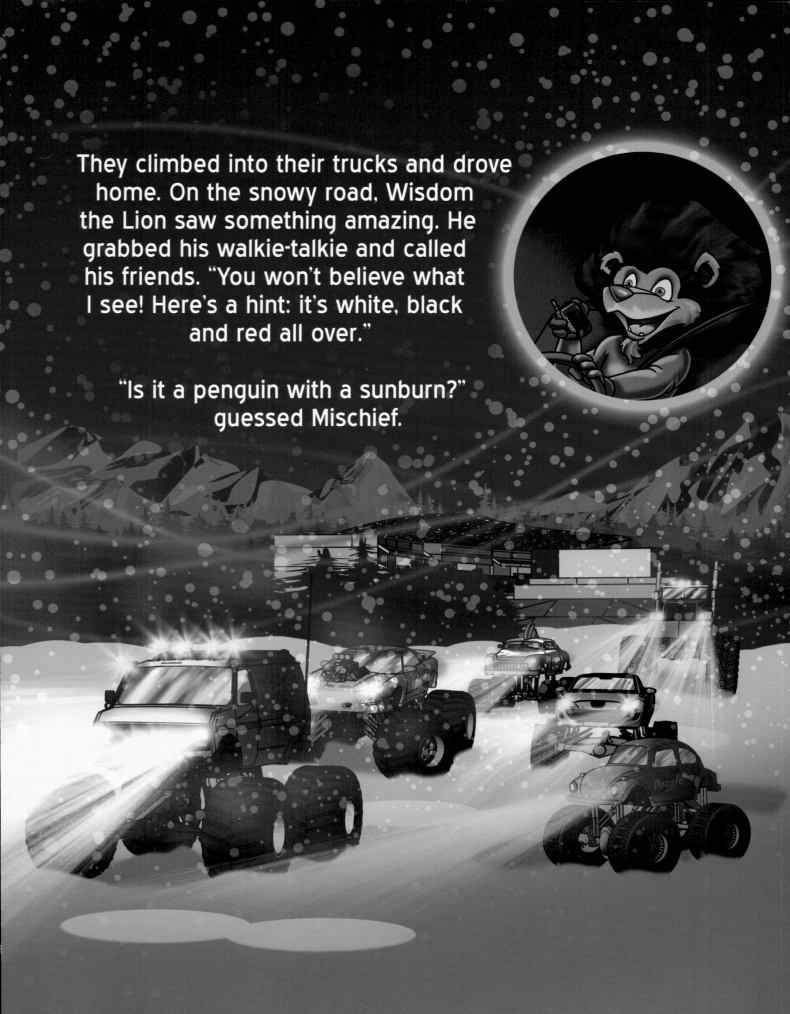

They climbed into their trucks and drove home. On the snowy road, Wisdom the Lion saw something amazing. He grabbed his walkie-talkie and called his friends. "You won't believe what I see! Here's a hint: it's white, black and red all over."

"Is it a penguin with a sunburn?" guessed Mischief.

"Nope," answered Wisdom. "It's Santa Claws!
But why is he sitting on the side of the road?"

Parking their trucks, they ran up to Santa, who didn't look jolly.

"Donner's gone, Dancer's waltzed away, Blitzen's blasted off . . . and now my sleigh won't fly," sighed Santa. "I can't deliver my last presents." He took off his hat—Santa had given up.

Wisdom inspected the sleigh. Christmas morning was only a few hours away. "I think we can help, but we have to hurry," said the smart lion.

The X-tails ran around picking up presents—round ones, square ones and even bicycle-shaped ones. Then they dragged the sleigh down the road.

At home, they worked in the garage.

"No peeking, Santa. We want to surprise you," said Dazzle the Bear, turning a wrench.

Crash sprayed paint, but mostly on himself!

And Wisdom worked on a top-secret gadget. At last, the sleigh was fixed.

"What do you think?" asked Charm.
Santa put his hat back on.
He looked at the X-tails and shouted,

"HO, HO, HO!

If we all pitch in, we can save Christmas in X-ville!"

Santa handed out pieces of his list. "Let's get to work," he said. "Now don't forget . . . you have to be as quiet as a mouse."

They split up and drove their monster trucks through the deep snow.

Going from house to house, Santa didn't make a peep, not even a squeak. He was a perfect sneak.

But it was not a silent night for the X-tails.

CLANK ... CLUNK ... CRASH!

"Oops, who put that there?" said the tangled hippo,
knocking over a Christmas tree.

"**RRRRR!** Come back here you BEARGLAR!" barked a guard dog, chasing after Dazzle.

weeeoooo . . . weeeoooo . . . weeeoooo . . .

wailed a house alarm.

"Don't mind me. I'm just helping out Santa.
Really, I'm not 'lion'," laughed Wisdom.

"OHHHH, I'm SOOOO full from milk and cookies. How does Santa fit in these chimneys?" wondered Flight the Gorilla, who was stuck.

Mischief slid down a chimney, but he didn't notice the smoke. "My bunwiches are burning!" he howled.

"aHHHH, that feels much better!"

Charm had been busy, delivering tons of presents. She arrived at her last house and pulled out gifts for the mommy and daddy. Charm reached for another present, but her bag was empty!

Looking at her list and checking it twice, there was only one name left—Leap. "Oh no," she thought. "I'm missing a present. What should I do?"

Suddenly, she knew the answer and hopped out the front door.

Hours later, they were done. Tired but happy, the X-tails and Santa high-fived.

"I can't believe we delivered so many presents," said Dazzle. "And look, it stopped snowing. I see the moon. I see stars. I see a Comet . . . a Donner and a Rudolph! I see the reindeer!"

Wasting no time, Santa shouted their reindeer names. No luck.

He tried whistling.

He even waved his arms and danced around. Nothing worked. The reindeer were too far away.

"It's a wacky idea, but could I use the high jump?" asked Santa. "I've got to reach them!"

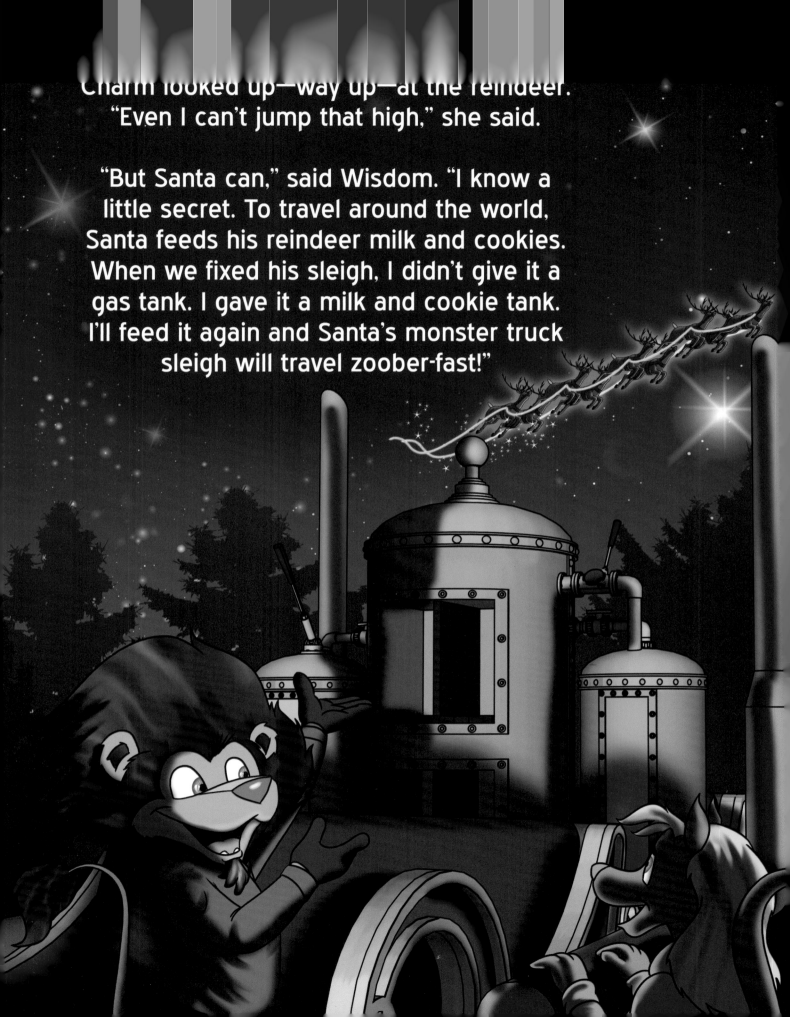

Charm looked up—way up—at the reindeer. "Even I can't jump that high," she said.

"But Santa can," said Wisdom. "I know a little secret. To travel around the world, Santa feeds his reindeer milk and cookies. When we fixed his sleigh, I didn't give it a gas tank. I gave it a milk and cookie tank. I'll feed it again and Santa's monster truck sleigh will travel zoober-fast!"

"Thank you, Charm," said Santa. "Merci, Dazzle. You're the best, Mischief. Couldn't have done it without you, Wisdom. Take it easy, Crash. Stay zoober-cool, Flight."

Santa sped away, shouting joyfully.

"HO, HO, HO!

To the North Pole I go!"

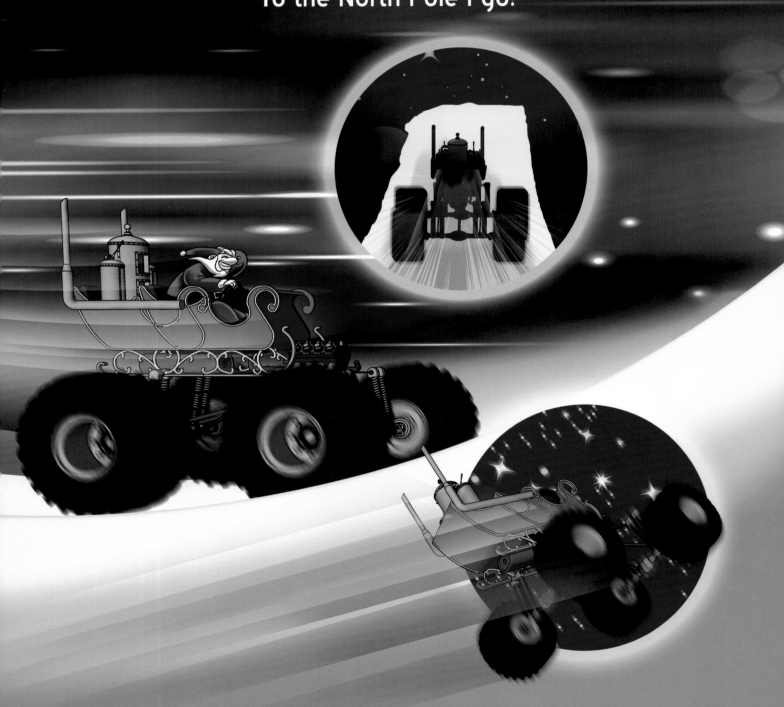

He drove off the high jump, flying over the town and towards the moon—closer and closer to his reindeer. One more whistle! They heard it and flew to him. Santa caught his rascally reindeer!

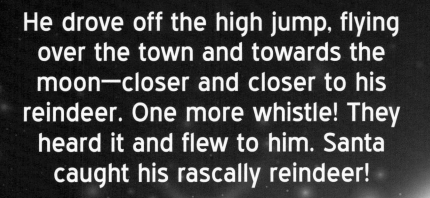

The X-tails waved up at Santa, who was gone in a flash.

Flight stopped. "Wait a sec. Did anyone deliver presents to our house?"

"NONE. ZILCH. NUTHIN'. ZIPPO. DIDDLY SQUAT,"

answered the rest of the X-tails.

"Maybe our presents were lost when Santa crashed," said Charm. "That's okay. Tonight I learned it's more fun to give presents than get them. I gave my magic present to a little rabbit named Leap."

When the X-tails arrived home, there was
a surprise under their tree.

"Wow!" said Mischief.
"Everyone in X-ville
got presents—even
us. We were the
best little helpers.
And just like
Santa said, we
were as quiet
as a moose."

They laughed
till their
bellies
ached!

Christmas was saved. At Leap's house, all was peaceful—but not for long. The little rabbit woke up and zoomed to the tree.

His parents were already there, sipping carrot tea. Leap picked up a present with his name on it. He excitedly ripped the wrapping paper, uncovering an empty snow globe. Giving it a shake, the snow swirled around and something magical appeared.

"Hey, is that me in a monster truck? Awesome! This is the best Christmas ever!" said Leap.

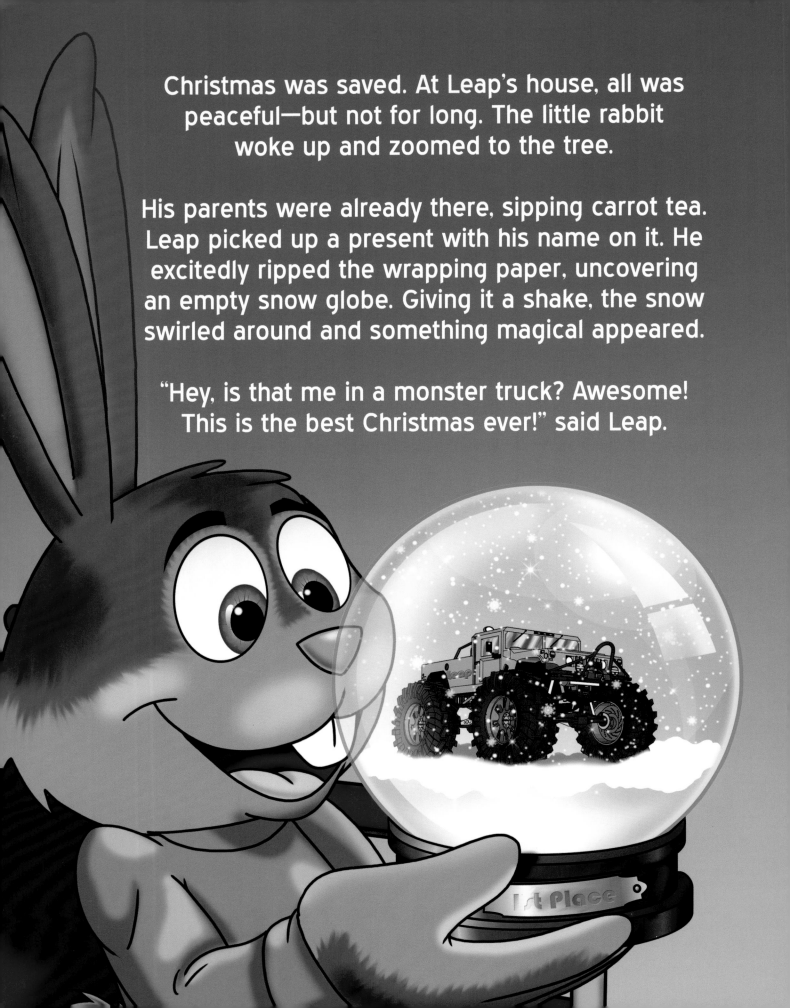

His daddy thought it was the best Christmas, too—especially when he looked out the window. His eyes opened wide. "Oh, Leap. There's one more present for you."

L.A. FIELDING

is an author of children's literature and a member of the Canadian Authors Association. He dreamed up the X-tails for his two children, while telling stories on their long distance trips to the mountains each winter weekend. It is his family's cozy log home in Prince George, British Columbia, and their Fielding Shred Shack at a local ski resort, where he draws his inspiration.

Growing up skateboarding, biking, and snowboarding, L.A. Fielding now shares the fun of those sports with his family. When not writing or telling stories, he focuses his thoughts on forestry as a Registered Professional Forester. *The X-tails in a Merry Monster Trucking Christmas* is his eighth book in the X-tails series.

Other books in the series include:

- *The X-tails Snowboard at Shred Park*
- *The X-tails Skateboard at Monster Ramp*
- *The X-tails Ski at Spider Ridge*
- *The X-tails BMX at Thunder Track*
- *The X-tails Surf at Shark Bay*
- *The X-tails Travel to the Jamboree Jam*
- *The X-tails Dirt Bike at Badlands*

WWW.THEXTAILS.COM